Cambridge
Early Years

Let's Explore

Learner's Book 2C

Kathryn Harper & Elly Schottman

Contents

Note to parents and practitioners   3

Block 5: Growing   4

Block 6: Animals   18

Acknowledgements   32

Note to parents and practitioners

This Learner's Book provides activities to support the third term of Let's Explore for Cambridge Early Years 2.

Activities can be used at school or at home. Children will need support from an adult. Additional guidance about activities can be found in the **For practitioners** boxes.

Some activities use stickers. The stickers can be found in the section in the middle of this book.

Stories are provided for children to enjoy looking at and listening to. Children are not expected to be able to read the stories themselves.

Children will encounter the following characters within this book. You could ask children to point to the characters when they see them on the pages, and say their names.

The Learner's Book activities support the Teaching Resource activities. The Teaching Resource provides step-by-step coverage of the Cambridge Early Years curriculum and guidance on how the Learner's Book activities develop the curriculum learning statements.

Hi, my name is Mia.

Find us on the front covers doing lots of fun activities.

Hi, my name is Gemi.

Hi, my name is Rafi.

Hi, my name is Kiho.

For practitioners
Children explore the picture and discuss what they can see. Children stick the matching pictures in place, e.g., grapes to grape vine. Encourage children to name the edible parts of plants they see and describe what the people in the picture are doing. Ask *What do plants needs to grow? (water and light)*. Encourage children to find Mia in the picture.

A little seed

Read and write.

Put the pictures in order.

Out comes the sun, yellow and round.

Up, up, up! The seed begins to grow!

I'm a little seed in the dark, dark ground.

Down comes the cool rain, soft and slow.

For practitioners

Explain that the pictures are not in the correct order. Point to the picture with the traceable number 1 and read the words, encouraging children to repeat after you. Say *Look at the seed in the other pictures. Which picture and words come next? How has the seed changed?* Children write numbers 1–4 to show the correct order of the 4 pictures.

Leaves and flowers

Read and draw.

What colour flowers do you see in the picture?

_____

_____

_____

Draw a line to a leaf that looks like this: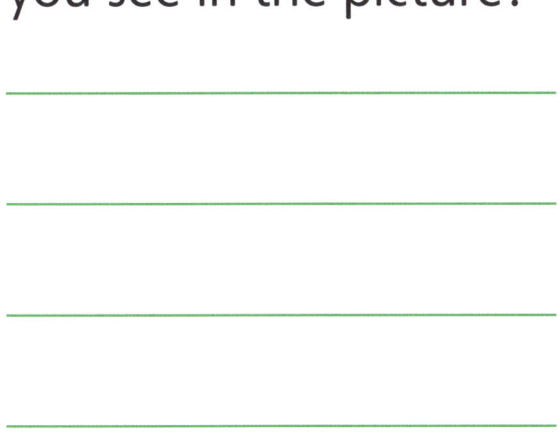

Draw a yellow flower.

For practitioners
Read the sentences together and encourage children to talk about the different colours and shapes they see in the image.

Watch my bean plant grow!
Draw and say.

Day ____

Day ____

Day ____

Day ____

For practitioners
Children make observational drawings of their bean plants four times over the course of three weeks. They use these pages to show how the plants have changed and grown over time. The first drawing should be made when the bean plants first emerge from the soil, or soon afterwards. This drawing can be labelled 'Day 1'. Keep track of the days that pass by posting the count on a sign in the Let's Explore Continuous provision area. Children refer to this sign as they label their subsequent drawings.

My special flower

Colour and say.

Choose 4 colours for the colouring key.
Colour the flower.

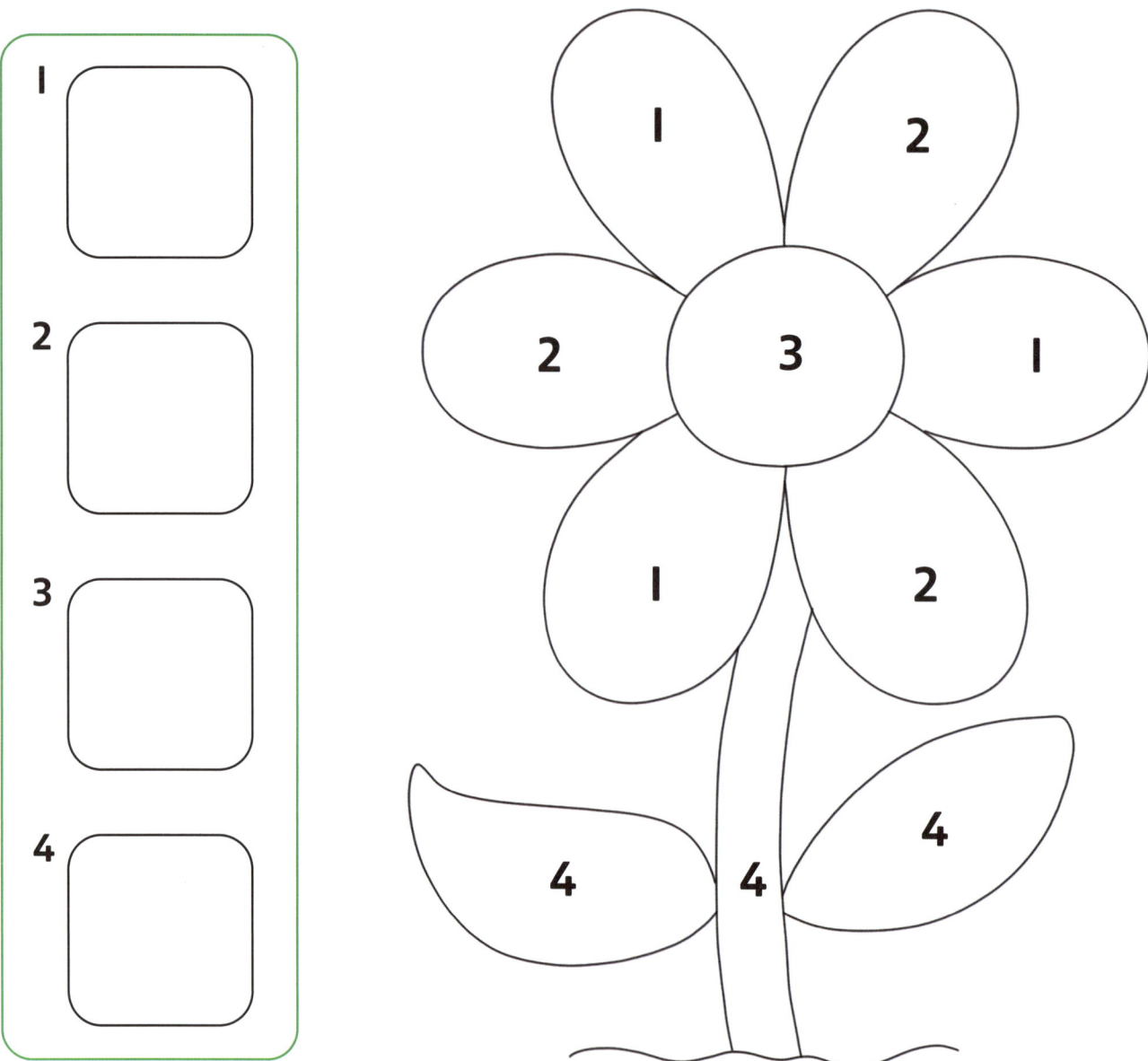

For practitioners
In pairs, children choose 4 colours for their colouring key, then colour the flower according to the numbers. Encourage children to discuss who will colour which part of the flower to ensure they are collaborating fairly. Once the pictures are coloured, children share their work with another pair and talk about what inspired them – it might have been a flower they saw in class this week.

Rough or smooth?
Touch and draw.

Rough	
Smooth	

For practitioners
Gather a variety of different fruits with either rough or smooth textures. Children take turns touching each fruit. Ask *Is it rough or smooth?* Encourage children to describe the texture of each fruit. Children then draw each fruit in the table in either the 'Rough' or the 'Smooth' row, depending on their texture.

How to make a sandwich

Draw.

Follow instructions and draw them.

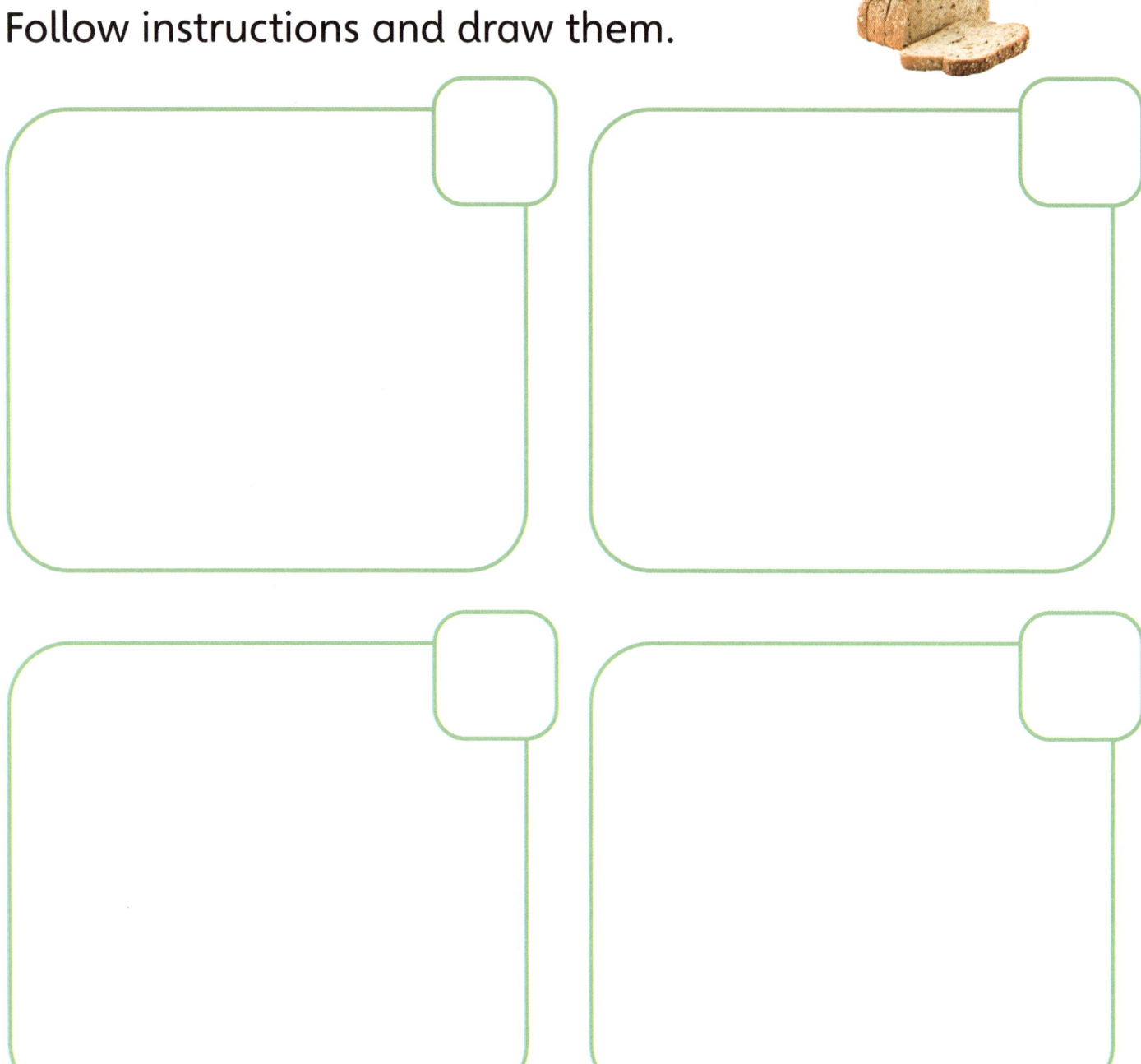

For practitioners

Have children name several favorite sandwiches and together act out the steps for making each sandwich. Ask *What do we do first? What do we do next? What else do we put on our sandwiches? And the last step is to eat our sandwiches!* Children then draw each step of how to make a sandwich in the boxes and number them 1–4.

Parts of a tree
Draw.

For practitioners
Take children to find tree leaves outside, or provide a range of different tree leaves. Each child chooses a leaf. Ask children to look closely and describe what they see. What shape and colour is it? What can they see on the leaf? What does it feel like? Children draw their leaf with as much detail as possible. Then talk about the different parts of a tree, using the image in the top left corner to help prompt conversation.

What's made of wood?
Circle.

For practitioners
Children circle the objects that are made of wood. Discuss their answers together. Do they know what the other objects are made from? Ask *Why is wood better than another material to make these objects?*

What can babies do?

Match and say.

Draw lines from the words to the babies doing those actions.

crawl   clap   cry   sit   wave   hug

For practitioners

Talk about the actions and movements in the pictures. Ask *What are the babies doing?* Encourage children to use the activity-specific vocabulary provided in the word labels as well as other descriptive words. Read the words and ask children to draw a line from each word to the baby or babies doing that action.

Can you do it?

Mark and say.

Try each challenge! Tick ✔ the boxes.

Stand on one foot. Count to 4.

Can you do it?

Yes, I can! ☐   No, not yet. ☐

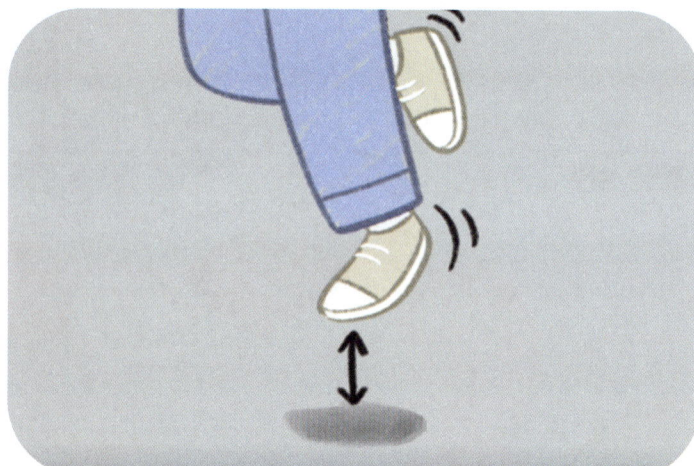

Hop on one foot 5 times.

Can you do it?

Yes, I can! ☐   No, not yet. ☐

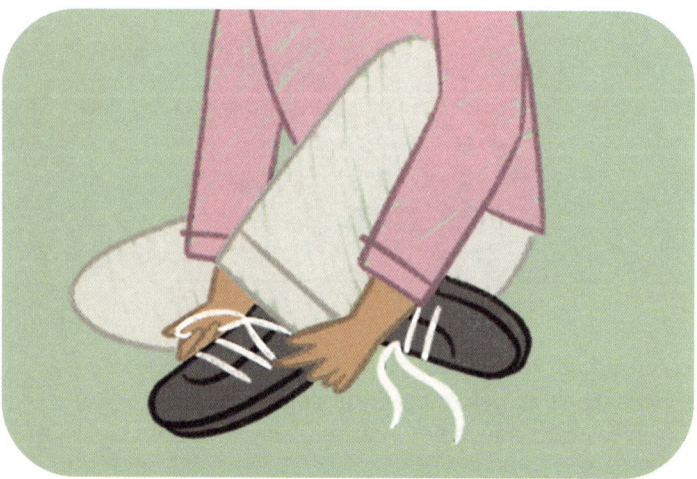

Tie your shoe.

Can you do it?

Yes, I can! ☐   No, not yet. ☐

Touch your nose to your knee.

Can you do it?

Yes, I can! ☐   No, not yet. ☐

Pat your head and rub your tummy.

Can you do it?

Yes, I can! ☐   No, not yet. ☐

Draw a star.

Can you do it?

Yes, I can! ☐   No, not yet. ☐

For practitioners

Read each challenge together and let children tick if they can do it now or not yet. Encourage children to talk about other physical actions that they are learning to do. Ask them to show you these movements. Ask *Can babies do these things too? What about adults?*

Block 6 Animals

Can you see the animals?
Choose stickers and say.

For practitioners
Children explore the picture and discuss what they can see. Children stick the matching pictures in place, e.g., monkey to tree. Explore the picture together and ask *Have you seen any of these animals?* Talk about the animals including what they look like, how they move, what noise they make. Ask children if they know what animals come out at night. Encourage children to find Gemi in the picture.

What's your favourite animal?
Draw and say.

My favourite animal is _____.

For practitioners
Children draw and colour their favourite animal. They can write what the animal is with assistance where necessary. In pairs, ask children to take turns asking each other questions about their animal such as *Why do you like them? Why are they special? What noises do they make? How do they move?* Encourage children to share something about their favourite animal with the class.

Animal coats
Match and colour.

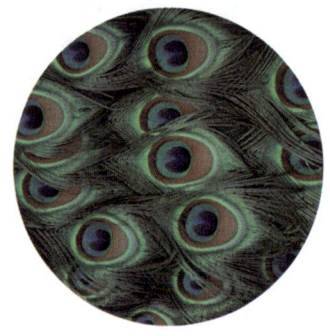

For practitioners
Children examine the different patterns and try to describe them. They then match them to the animals and colour the animals in. Discuss each of the animal patterns and ask *Do they look soft to touch? What colours are they? Can you see any stripes?*

What noises do they make?
Circle.

loud   quiet

loud   quiet

loud   quiet

loud   quiet

For practitioners
Review the terms *loud* and *quiet*, reminding children what each one means and that they relate to volume. Make sure they know which word is loud and which word is quiet. Children look at the animals and circle the word that most closely applies. They can try to make the sound.

Make an animal dance

Move.

Animals:

1	rabbit	parrot	otter
2	monkey	kangaroo	rabbit
3	parrot	otter	monkey
4	kangaroo	monkey	rabbit

Dance to some music!

For practitioners

Ask children to identify the animals and show you how each animal moves. Children then choose a row from the table and perform each animal movement in the row as a sequence. You could play music in the background. Encourage them to think of different movements the animal might do, e.g., monkey – scratch head, swing through the trees.

What's wrong with the pictures?
Circle and say.

For practitioners

Start by reviewing what we can expect to see in the day and at night. How is the light different? The sky? The animals? For example, sometimes you can see the moon while the mun is still out. Talk about the animals that are active in the daytime and the nighttime, reminding children of the word nocturnal. Ask *Are bats nocturnal?* Children then examine each picture in turn and circle the part of the picture that doesn't belong, such as stars in a blue sky.

Where do they live?
Match.

For practitioners
Point to and talk about the different habitats. Discuss what is similar and different about them. Talk about the animals and where they might live. Children draw lines through the maze to match the habitat to the correct animal.

What have they got?
Tick ✓ and say.

	wings	fur	tail	feathers	claws	fins
a shark						
a bear						
a tiger						
a bird						
an elephant						

For practitioners
Show children how to move their fingers along the rows and identify the different columns. Talk about what each of the features along the top are. You could use toy animals from the Construction and small world play area to show an example of each feature. Children draw a tick or smiley face for the features the different animals have. Use the chart to compare the animals and identify similarities and differences. Talk about how the same features can look different on different animals, for example, an elephant's tail looks different from a shark's tail.

What do you like best?
Trace.

For practitioners
Children look at the pictures and trace the heart next to their favourite thing from each line. Discuss their choices. Use this to draw on the experiences and reflect on the knowledge children have developed throughout this block.

I'm a duckling!

Choose and tick.

Mummy duck

Six little ducks that I once knew
A white duck, yellow duck, green and blue.
But the Mummy duck with the feather on her back
She led the others with a quack, quack, quack.
Quack, quack, quack-quack, quack, quack
She led the others with a quack, quack, quack.

Down to the river they would go.
Wibble wobble, wibble wobble to and fro.
But the Mummy duck with the feather on her back
She led the others with a quack, quack, quack.
Quack, quack, quack-quack, quack, quack
She led the others with a quack, quack, quack.

Home from the river they would come.
Wibble wobble, wibble wobble, ho-hum-hum.
But the Mummy duck with the feather on her back
She led the others with a quack, quack, quack.
Quack, quack, quack-quack, quack, quack
She led the others with a quack, quack, quack.

hungry ☐   happy ☐   sleepy ☐   fast ☐

silly ☐   sad ☐   shy ☐   noisy ☐

Now sing and act out your duck.

For practitioners

As a class, talk about what actions children could do for each of the characteristics above. Ask *How can you show this with your face or body?* Children choose one of the ducks from the song: the white duck, yellow duck, green and blue duck, or the mummy duck. They think about the personality of their duck and tick the features – more than one is possible. They then sing and act as their duck in small groups.

Acknowledgements

The authors and publishers acknowledge the following sources of copyright material and are grateful for the permissions granted.
While every effort has been made, it has not always been possible to identify the sources of all the material used, or to trace all copyright holders.
If any omissions are brought to our notice, we will be happy to include the appropriate acknowledgements on reprinting.

Thanks to the following for permission to reproduce images:

p7 wjarek/GI; p12 fcafotodigital/GI, Yevgen Romanenko/GI, HUIZENG HU/GI; p14 ilbusca/GI, domin_domin/GI, MirageC/GI, Francesco Milanese/GI, ThomasVogel/GI, AaronAmat/GI, IgorKovalchuk/GI, dlerick/GI, Devonyu/GI; p21 Image Source/GI, Martin Barraud/GI, Jami Tarris/GI, Richard Olivier/GI; p22 Martin Harvey/GI, Jeny S/GI, Digital Zoo/GI, GarysFRP/GI; p23 bradleyblackburn/GI, MediaProduction/GI, GlobalP/GI, GlobalP/GI, GlobalP/GI; p24 sodar99/GI, John Twynam/GI, Nora Carol Photography/GI, Sebastian Condrea/GI, goldhafen/GI, Alexey_Seafarer/GI, vusta/GI, nizha2/GI; p27 bbevren/GI, JackF/GI, luamduan/GI, GlobalP/GI, Petr Pikora//GI; p31 Benoit BACOU/GI, Michael Duva/GI, GlobalP/GI, Fernando Trabanco Fotografia/GI, Pakhnyushchyy/GI, GlobalP/GI, Yaorusheng/GI, Jose A. Bernat Bacete/GI, eugenesergeev/GI, Kelvin Murray/GI, czekma13/GI, Senez Studio/GI

Thanks to the following artists at Beehive Illustration:

Lays Bittencourt, Veronika Chaves, Chloe Evans, Helen Graper, Tamara Joubert, Michelle McGovern, Sarah Pitt, Jan Smith, Joe Wilkins.

Cover characters by Becky Davies (The Bright Agency)